ISOBEL'S STANLEY CUP

ISOBEL'S STANLEY CUP

Kristin Butcher

CP | CRWTH PRESS

Library and Archives Canada Cataloguing in Publication

Butcher, Kristin, author
Isobel's Stanley Cup / Kristin Butcher.

Issued in print and electronic formats.
ISBN 978-1-77533-196-4 (softcover).—ISBN 978-1-77533-194-0 (PDF).
—ISBN 978-1-77533-195-7 (EPUB).

I. Title.
PS8553.U6972I86 2018   jC813⸴.54
C2018-903614-1
C2018-903615-X

Summary

Isobel Harkness wants to play hockey like her hero Isobel Stanley,
but it's 1893 and her father doesn't believe hockey is a sport for girls.

This interior of this book is printed on 100% post-consumer waste paper.
The cover stock is FSC certified.

Cover art by Kasio Charko • Interior illustrations by Kristin Butcher
Cover and interior design by Julia Breese

Crwth Press
#204 – 2320 Woodland Drive
Vancouver, BC V5N 3P2
www.crwth.ca
Printed and bound in Canada
21 20 19 18 · 4 3 2 1

*For Don Cherry and Ron MacLean, who
provided the inspiration for Isobel's story.*

PAPA SAYS NO

Isobel circled the dining table, banging down knives and forks and throwing the napkins onto the plates. She could hear her brothers in the other room. She could smell them too. Well, not them, exactly. But she could smell the fresh winter air they had brought indoors after their snowball fight.

She had watched them through the window as she'd dusted the sitting room.

It looked like such fun. She had wanted to play too. But according to Papa, throwing snowballs wasn't a suitable activity for a young lady. Neither was hockey, and Isobel wanted to do that more than anything.

She hated having to be a young lady. It was boring. Boys had all the fun.

Isobel might have been happier if she'd had a sister to do things with. But she didn't. All she had were five brothers. To make matters worse, they were all older.

She sighed. All she ever got to do was help her mother with chores. It was so unfair. She didn't want to embroider pillow slips and fold laundry. She wanted to play hockey with her brothers.

As she put out the water glasses, she made her mind up. She would ask Papa one more time.

Isobel glared at the newspaper hiding her father's face.

"It's not fair!" She pouted.

Mama shook her head in warning, and Isobel's brothers stopped eating. Their eyes bugged out as they stared at their little sister. No one ever spoke back to Papa.

Papa lowered his *Ottawa Citizen* and put it down beside his plate. Then he took off his spectacles and laid them down too.

He frowned at Isobel. "The world is not always fair, Isobel. You will find that out soon enough. But this is not about fairness. It's about what is proper. Some activities are meant for boys and some for girls. It's as simple as that. Hockey is a boys' game. It is not suitable for young ladies."

"Why not?" Isobel demanded. "I can skate as good as Billy and Matt."

"As *well* as Billy and Matt," her mother corrected her.

Isobel heaved a frustrated sigh. "As *well* as Billy and Matt. So why shouldn't I be allowed to play?"

"You might get hurt," her father said. "Hockey is a rough sport."

"I'm not going to break, Papa. I'm fit and strong. Just yesterday I beat Billy at arm wrestling."

"I let you win," Billy blustered.

"You did not," Isobel retorted. "I beat you fair and square, Billy Harkness!"

"Children, stop," Mama said. "There will be no squabbling at the dinner table."

"And there will be no more arm wrestling either, Isobel," Papa added. He sent his daughter a look that meant the subject was closed. Then he turned to his wife. "It is obvious that Isobel is spending too much time with her brothers. Is there not something else she could do? Read poetry? Paint? Take singing lessons, perhaps?"

The mere thought made Isobel shudder. "Isobel Stanley plays hockey." She flung the words at her father like a dare. "I saw her picture in the newspaper. She plays with other young women on the rink at Rideau Hall. If the Governor General's daughter can play hockey, why can't I?"

"Isobel, that's quite enough," Mama scolded her.

Papa cleared his throat and picked up his knife and fork. "Listen to your mother, child. How Lord Stanley runs his family is his business. It has nothing to do with how I run mine. You may continue to skate, but there will be no more talk of hockey. Is that clear?"

Isobel scowled. It was clear all right. But she didn't have to like it.

HOCKEY LESSONS

The ice rink was a flooded field on Ossington Avenue. Isobel's brothers and the other boys who lived on the street thought of it as their personal property. But anyone could skate there—even girls.

Isobel glided around the edges of the ice. She was careful to stay out of the way of the boys who were practising for a game that afternoon.

They would be playing the Seneca Street team. Most of those boys were older and bigger. Isobel wasn't willing to admit they were better, though.

Her brothers were all very good players. Alexander, who was fourteen and the oldest, had a fierce shot. The twins, Freddie and John, were thirteen and could skate like the wind. Matt, at eleven, won almost every faceoff. And Billy, who was ten—only a year older than Isobel and not even an inch taller—could stickhandle around players as if they were standing still.

The other boys on their team, Jamie, Robert, and Simon, were good too. Even so, the Ossington team had never beaten the Senecca boys.

When the Seneca team arrived, Isobel's brothers and their teammates left the ice so the other boys could warm up before the game.

"Back away, Isobel," Alexander said. "And keep your eyes open. You don't want to get hit by the puck."

"Look out!" she yelled. A hockey stick was zinging straight for his head! She dove at him, sending them both sprawling. The stick shot harmlessly into a snowbank.

"You're the one who should keep your eyes open," Isobel told her brother.

"Sorry about that." A big boy on the other team waved and shrugged. "The stick slipped out of my hands."

"I don't think he's sorry at all," Isobel grumbled. "I think he did that on purpose."

———•———

It was a close game. The Ossington Avenue boys played better than they ever had before. With just a few minutes left, they were winning 3–2.

Excited and hopeful, Isobel cheered loudly from the sidelines. If she had any voice left when the game was over, it would be a miracle.

"Come on, Ossington!" she shouted. "You can do it."

Someone shot the puck across the ice. The boy who had nearly taken Alexander's head off earlier was chasing it. Suddenly he slipped, and down he went.

His stick flew out of his hands, and he slid into a snowbank. He was so close to Isobel she could have touched him.

She knew she should keep back. But she was caught up in the excitement of the game and couldn't help herself. She leaned over the snowbank. "How do you expect to win if you can't skate?" she teased. "Want me to teach you?"

The boy's eyes became angry slits, and his nostrils flared in and out. It was not a friendly face. Isobel stepped back.

"Hurry, Harry. Get the puck," one of the Seneca players called.

"This game isn't over, little girl," the boy named Harry growled. "We'll see what a smarty-pants you are when your team loses." Then he pushed himself up, retrieved his stick, and skated away with the puck.

Freddie was waiting for him. But when Freddie tried to take the puck away, Harry hit him hard on the shin with his stick. Isobel gasped as Freddie sank to the ice, holding his leg and groaning.

It was John's turn to chase Harry. He would have had him, too, if a player on the other team hadn't tripped John from behind.

"Hey!" Isobel cried. "That's not fair."

But nobody heard her over all the cheering. The Seneca boys had scored.

The game was tied.

With time running out, the teams quickly lined up for the faceoff. Matt won it and passed the puck to Billy.

Right away, Billy was zigzagging around the players. And then, *BAM!* Somebody elbowed him in the face so hard it knocked him on his back!

Before Isobel had time to blink, the Seneca team stole the puck and scored.

The boy keeping time whistled. The game was over.

"They shouldn't have won," Isobel protested after the other team left.

Alexander shrugged. "We'll get them next time."

"How? They'll just cheat again."

Her brother pinched her cheek and grinned. "We'll get tougher and trickier. We'll outsmart them. Right, boys?"

"Right!" They all cheered.

"You can help, Isobel," Alexander said.

"Me? What can I do?"

"When we practise, you can pretend you're the other team. Do every dirty trick you can think of, and we'll figure out how to outsmart you."

"But Papa said I'm not allowed to play hockey."

"You won't be playing," Alexander said. "Not really. It's more like you'll be coaching. Papa didn't say anything about that." He winked.

Isobel winked back and grinned. "No, he didn't."

———•———

The team practised every day, and Isobel practised with them. It took a while for her to get used to skating with a stick. But soon it felt like a part of her body.

She didn't like the idea of hooking the boys or tripping them. But Alexander was right. It did help them improve their play. Isobel had to work harder and harder to catch them.

Though she didn't realize it, Isobel was also improving. Her legs got stronger. Her skating got faster. When she got the puck, it was harder for the boys to steal it back. Soon Isobel could weave through players almost as well as Billy.

"Let's see what you can do with team-mates, Isobel," Alexander said one day. He divided the players—including Isobel—into two sides. "Now we'll see if you can pass and shoot."

After that, Isobel played at every prac-tice. And she got better and better. The boys noticed.

"You know, Isobel," Billy said as they walked home from practice one day, "for somebody who doesn't play hockey, you're pretty good."

ISOBEL MEETS ISOBEL

Isobel looked forward to watching the weekly hockey games. But one Saturday, Mama had other plans.

"I'll miss the boys' game," Isobel protested. "They need me to cheer them on."

"There will be other games, Isobel," her mother said. "I'm sure the boys can manage without you this one time. We've already put off this shopping trip for too long. And you've been growing like a weed. If we don't get you a new coat and boots, you'll be stuck inside until spring."

Isobel sighed. There was no point in arguing. Besides, her mother was right. No matter how much she tugged at the sleeves of her coat, they no longer covered her wrists. And her toes hurt from being stuffed inside her boots.

Mama stroked Isobel's hair and smiled. "We'll make a day of it—just you and me. After we've done our shopping, we'll have lunch at a restaurant. Would you like that?"

Isobel nodded.

"And we can take our skates," her mother added. "We'll pass right by the rink outside Rideau Hall. We could go for a skate. Doesn't that sound like fun?"

Isobel had to admit that it did.

Mama finished lacing up her skates. She puffed her cheeks out and patted her tummy.

"I ate too much," she said. "I feel like a walrus."

"A skating walrus." Isobel grinned at the image that popped into her head. "Come on, Mama. I'll race you across the ice."

Mama was fun to skate with—not stuffy or proper like so many other ladies on the ice. She skated forwards and backwards with ease. She even joined Isobel in a game of tag. When she finally left the ice, her cheeks were rosy and her eyes were sparkling.

"That was great fun," she said.

"You're a good skater, Mama," Isobel told her. "Where did you learn?"

Mama smiled. "I had brothers too Isobel. And before you children were born, your father and I often came here to skate."

Isobel's mouth fell open. "Papa can skate?"

Mama nodded. "He hasn't in years, but he can. Oh, look, Isobel." She nodded towards the ice. "There's a hockey game starting."

Sure enough, there was. And it was ladies playing!

Isobel spotted a player dressed all in white. She stood out like a beacon among the other ladies in their dark clothing.

"It's Isobel Stanley!" Isobel exclaimed. "Oh, Mama. Can I—I mean, may I—watch her? Please. Just for a little while?"

Mama shrugged. "I don't see why not. We have time."

Isobel was over the moon. Though there were fourteen young women playing hockey, she couldn't take her eyes off Isobel Stanley. She was the best player on the ice.

She could skate and shoot every bit as well as any boy. She scored two goals while Isobel was watching. How Isobel wished she could play hockey like Isobel Stanley.

Then the most wonderful thing happened. Halfway through the game there was a rest period, and the players left the ice. Isobel Stanley came and stood right beside Isobel!

She smiled, so Isobel smiled back.

"Do you like hockey?" asked Isobel Stanley.

Isobel tried to speak. But she was so in awe of the young woman standing beside her, the words wouldn't come out. All she could do was nod.

"Do you play?"

Isobel almost nodded again. But she didn't want Miss Stanley to think she didn't know how to talk. She reached deep inside herself. She had to have words somewhere. She looked down the ice. Mama waved.

Then she looked back at Isobel Stanley. "Yes," she whispered. "But it's a secret."

Isobel Stanley's eyebrows shot up. "A secret?"

Isobel bobbed her head. "My papa doesn't approve of girls playing hockey." She clapped a hand over her mouth. What if Miss Stanley was insulted?

Isobel Stanley laughed. "That's all right. A lot of people feel that way. But times are changing, and so are ideas. My father didn't want me to play hockey at first. Be patient.

I'm sure your papa will change his thinking. Who do you play with?"

"My brothers. But only when they practise. One of the teams they play against has older boys, and they are mean. They trip and hit and do other dirty tricks. I pretend I'm them, so my brothers can practise avoiding them."

"Well," said Isobel Stanley, her eyebrows knotted together in thought. "Can I make a suggestion?"

"Yes, please."

"It's hard to hit a moving target. The trick is to skate fast and not stop. If the other players can't catch your brothers, they can't hit them." She glanced towards the ice. The players were returning. "The game is starting again." She smiled and waved. "I have to go. Good luck!"

As Isobel Stanley skated away, Isobel thought about what she had said. Skate faster. It sounded simple enough, but would it work?

THE CHALLENGE

"It says here in the newspaper that the award Lord Stanley is donating to the Amateur Hockey Association of Canada's champions is due to arrive this spring,"

Papa said at dinner that night. "The challenge is open to all amateur hockey teams."

"Does that mean our Ossington Avenue team can try for it, Papa?" Billy asked.

John and Freddie hooted. "Not much chance of that," John said.

Billy went red in the face.

Alexander frowned at the twins and then turned to his youngest brother. "We probably could challenge for it, Billy, but there wouldn't be any point. The other teams would be men. We wouldn't stand a chance."

Papa continued, "This article says his children inspired him to donate the cup. They all like hockey and played it here in Canada."

"I bet anything it was Isobel Stanley who convinced her father to donate the cup," Isobel said. "She loves hockey as much as her brothers. She plays just as well too."

"Like you would know anything about it," Freddie scoffed.

Isobel stuck out her chin. "It just so happens that I do. I've seen her play."

All her brothers except Alexander burst into laughter.

"You're a liar," Billy sneered.

"I am not! Am I, Mama?"

"No, Isobel, you're not. And there will be no name calling, in any case. Is that under-stood, Billy?"

"Yes, Mama," Billy said, "but—"

"No buts." Mama cut him off sternly. Then she dabbed her mouth with her napkin.

"While Isobel and I were out today, we stopped at Rideau Hall for a skate. We saw Miss Stanley playing hockey. And Isobel is correct. She is very good."

Papa's spectacles almost fell off his nose as he gawked at his wife. "You went skating, Margaret?"

"Yes, Edward, I did. Is there something wrong with that?"

For a moment Papa just stared at Mama. Everyone else stared at Papa, wondering what he was going to say. Mama was the only one who continued eating her dinner.

Finally Papa shook his head and mumbled, "No, of course not" and went back to his newspaper.

Billy sighed. "I wish we could compete for it" he said.

"Perhaps you can one day." Mama smiled. "If you love the game enough, I'm sure you will."

"Well, *I* certainly will," Isobel announced.

Papa lowered a corner of his newspaper and frowned.

"Times are changing, Papa," she said. "I know it doesn't seem proper now for girls to play hockey, but it soon will. You'll see."

"Indeed," Papa said. "We shall see."

A GOOD IDEA

It was time for the Saturday afternoon hockey game. The Ossington team was playing the Seneca boys again. Isobel wasn't sure if she was looking forward to it or dreading it.

Her brothers' team had been practising really hard. But what if the other team played dirty again?

The game started well—good, clean hockey. Up and down the ice they went. Both sides had their chances, but into the second half of play, neither team had scored.

Isobel's fingers were crossed inside her mittens.

"Come on, boys! You can do it!"

Then Matt got the puck. He only had to get past one Seneca player and he'd have a clean shot at the goal.

"Come on, Matt! Come on, Matt!" Isobel cheered. "Skate hard. Go fast. You can beat him."

But instead of turning on the speed, Matt tried to stickhandle his way around the other player. He tried to make the Seneca boy go one way while he went another. It almost worked, too, but the Seneca player stuck out his leg and tripped Matt as he skated by.

Matt went down hard. When he didn't move, the other boys on the Ossington team hurried to see if he was hurt. That's when the Seneca team grabbed the puck, skated to the other end, and scored.

Alexander protested, but it didn't help. As far as the Seneca team was concerned, it was a good goal.

The game ended soon after that. And since no one else had scored, Seneca won again.

"We're never going to beat them," Billy grumbled as he took off his skates.

"Not with an attitude like that we won't," Alexander said.

"Not if they keep cheating, you mean," Isobel said. "Those boys play so dirty. We need a referee to keep things fair. I bet the teams trying for Lord Stanley's cup won't be allowed to cheat."

"Do you think Seneca could actually win without cheating?" Billy asked.

"We may never know." Matt sighed.

"Unless—" Isobel had an idea.

"Unless what, Isobel?" Alexander said.

"Unless we have a challenge tournament of our own. We could get some of the fathers to referee. They'll make sure the Seneca boys play fair."

"And what are we going to use for a prize?" John asked. "You can't have a tournament without something to win. Lord Stanley isn't going to buy another silver cup and donate it to us."

"Don't you worry about the prize, John Harkness," Isobel said. "I'll take care of that. The important thing is to set up the challenge games. We'll be the last team that's challenged."

"Do you think that's fair?" Alexander said.

Isobel shrugged. "Someone has to be last. Why not us? We're putting up the prize, and it's our idea."

Alexander nodded. "That's true."

"So how do we decide the order of the other challenges?" Freddie asked.

"We can draw names," Isobel suggested. "How many teams are there altogether?"

"Six, I think," Billy said.

"Seneca, of course," said Matt.

"And the Bank Street boys," John added.

"Don't forget Grosvenor and Wendover," Freddie chimed in.

"And Hopewell," his twin reminded him.

Billy screwed up his forehead in thought. "That makes five. There's one more. I'm sure of it."

"Yes, Billy. You're right," Alexander said. "There is one more." He paused, and then his face broke into a huge grin. "Ossington Avenue. Us." Everyone burst out laughing.

Billy blushed and smiled sheepishly. "Oh, yeah. I forgot."

MAMA TO THE RESCUE

Isobel had told the boys she would find a prize for the hockey challenge tournament. That was turning out to be a harder job than she had expected.

First, she looked through her own things. She had quite a few dolls and would have happily used one for the prize. But she was fairly certain none of the boys would want a doll—not even if she dressed it to look like a hockey player.

Then she thought of donating one of her books. But they were all for girls, and there were no girls on any of the teams.

The only thing that might have made a suitable prize was Isobel's Punch and Judy board game. But two of the playing cards were missing, so that was no good either.

Next, Isobel hunted through her brothers' things. They had toy soldiers, locomotives, wagons, animal figurines, building blocks, puzzles, and all sorts of other things boys liked. But what would be the point of winning the tournament if they were only going to get back what they already had?

No, she was going to have to come up with something else. Isobel thought of Lord Stanley's cup. She needed a prize like that.

But where could she get one? Even if she had the money—which she didn't— she couldn't go to England to buy a silver bowl. Not that it had to be silver. It could be wooden or glass. It didn't even have to be a bowl. A nice plate would do just fine. If Isobel painted hockey sticks on it, it would be perfect.

She wondered if Mama had something like that in her kitchen.

Isobel dug through cupboard after cupboard. In one she found spoons, bottles, funnels, and sieves. In another there were pots and roasting pans and platters of all sizes, but nothing that would make a good prize. A third cupboard was full of dinner plates, but they were decorated with flowers. That wouldn't work for a hockey prize.

When Mama came into the room, Isobel was sitting in the middle of the floor, surrounded by kitchen utensils.

"Isobel Harkness, what on earth are you doing?" Mama exclaimed as she took in the clutter.

Isobel looked around her, seeing the mess for the first time. She hung her head.

"Sorry, Mama," she said. "I was looking for something. I'll put everything back where it belongs."

"You most certainly will," Mama huffed. "What are you looking for, anyway? And why didn't you just ask me instead of rooting through the cupboards?"

"I'm trying to find a prize for the hockey challenge tournament."

Mama tilted her head, looking curious. "What tournament?"

Isobel explained, "The boys are setting up the challenge games and arranging referees. I'm supposed to find an award for the winning team. I wanted something like Lord Stanley's cup. But I can't find anything."

"Hmm … ," Mama said. "Hmm …" Finally, she bent down and started gathering the kitchen utensils. "I might have an idea. Let's get these things put away, and then we'll see what we can find."

———·———

"It's wonderful!" Isobel beamed. "Can I—I mean, *may* I—really have it for the prize?"

Mama examined the two-handled silver sugar bowl from various angles.

"It's tarnished," she said. "It needs a good polishing, that's for certain. And it's small—nowhere near as large as Lord Stanley's cup. But if you think it'll do the trick, Isobel, you're welcome to it. I don't have the matching creamer, so the sugar bowl is no use to me." She held it out. "Here you go. Now all you have to do is polish it. Let's get you set up."

Mama boiled some water and poured it into a large china bowl. Into that she spooned some baking soda and scraped in some dish soap. Then she whisked the water until soap bubbles appeared.

"All right, Isobel," she said, "place the sugar bowl in the water. But be careful. It's hot."

"Now what?" Isobel asked when the sugar bowl was submerged.

"Just watch," her mother said, swishing the water.

After a few minutes, Isobel said, "The water is getting dirty."

"So it is." Mama smiled. "But I think it could use a bit more help."

She went down to the cellar and returned with a jar of lemon juice and another of vinegar. Then she poured a little of each into the bowl of water.

"Oh!" Isobel exclaimed as the water began to fizz. "What's it doing?"

"It's eating away the tarnish on the sugar bowl," Mama explained. Once she deemed the bowl clean, she gave Isobel a soft, clean cloth. "You can shine it up with this," she said.

"It's beautiful," Isobel murmured when she was done.

"Yes, it is," Mama agreed. "Now it only needs a base to stand on. I think I know just the thing."

Down to the cellar she went again. When she came back, she had a pyramid of wooden blocks. "It's the base of an old lamp," she said. "I've always disliked it, but it's perfect for your challenge cup to sit on. We'll just paint it up and glue the sugar bowl on top."

She placed the sugar bowl on the pyramid and held it up in the air. "What do you think?"

Isobel grinned and clapped her hands. "It's perfect."

THE CHALLENGE TOURNAMENT

The challenge tournament consisted of five games. It took two full weekends plus one more Saturday to play them.

The first challenge was between Wendover and Hopewell. Wendover won easily. They won the next challenge against Grosvenor, too. But then they had to face Seneca, who defeated them 7–2. Now Bank Street was the only team standing between Seneca and Ossington.

The Bank Street boys gave it a good try, but Seneca was too much for them.

Isobel was surprised at how cleanly Seneca played. Except for one tripping incident, which even Isobel had to admit might have been accidental, they played a fair game. Having an adult referee seemed to be working.

Since the Ossington Avenue team was the last challenge, the boys had to fit their practices around the tournament matches. It wasn't the same as actually playing a game, but the boys did everything they could to get ready.

Isobel told them what Isobel Stanley had said about staying on the move and skating fast. So they had skating races. They played tag, and everyone tried to catch the person with the puck.

They practised their stickhandling and moving the puck to each other in combination plays. They also worked on their shooting, so that Jamie Barnes, the goalkeeper, got some practice too.

Isobel felt happy and proud to help. If only she could play in the big game.

———— · ————

The morning of the final challenge, she awoke to butterflies in her stomach.

This was it. It was Ossington's last chance to defeat Seneca. If they didn't, Seneca would be the champions—and they'd have a shiny silver challenge cup to prove it.

Isobel and the boys went for a morning skate before the game.

"Simon's sick!" Jamie said breathlessly as he ran up to them at the rink. "Bronchitis, his mom says. He won't be able to play."

Everyone looked at each other. Alexander frowned. "That leaves us with only seven players, including you in goal, Jamie. We have no spare. If someone gets hurt, we're done for."

Isobel felt the mood of the boys change. They were starting to worry.

"Don't even think about that," she said. "Nothing's going to happen—except we're finally going to beat Seneca. At least, we are if we get some practice in. Come on. Let's get our skates on."

It was a good practice. When it was over, everyone was in high spirits again. The children laughed and chattered all the way home.

Mama was waiting for them in the kitchen.

"Are you coming to the game this afternoon, Mama?" Isobel asked.

"I wouldn't miss it," Mama said with a smile. "Your papa's coming too. He had some errands to run this morning, but he will be back after lunch. Then we'll head straight for the game."

Isobel was surprised but pleased. "The more fans we have, the better," she said, beaming.

"I have something for you all," Mama said, reaching down beside the wood stove for her knitting bag. She plunked it on a chair.

"What is it?" Billy asked. He eyed the bag curiously.

Mama's eyes twinkled as she reached inside. "Toques," she said, pulling a handful of red knitted caps from the bag. "So you can see each other easily on the ice."

"Oh, Mama!" Freddie exclaimed. "These are great."

Mama passed out the woollen caps, and the boys pulled them onto their heads, grinning.

Isobel clapped her hands. "This is so wonderful! Now you really look like a team."

Mama handed three more caps to Alexander. "These are for Simon, Robert, and Jamie," she said.

"Simon is sick," Alexander told her. "He won't be playing today."

"Well, give it to him when he's feeling better," Mama said. Then she reached into the bag again and turned to Isobel. "And this one is for you, Isobel. As Ossington's number one supporter, you need a cap too."

AND THE WINNER IS ...

Lunch was noisy. The children were more excited than hungry, and everyone talked over each other. If Papa had been there, he would have glowered them into silence. But Mama didn't scold anyone.

At the end of the meal, Billy jumped up to demonstrate how he was going to stick-handle his way through the Seneca team and score the winning goal.

With his hat pulled down over his ears, he bent over his imaginary stick. He bounced from foot to foot as he pretended to weave through the players.

Everyone laughed.

And then something terrible happened. While bobbing about, Billy came down awkwardly on his foot. It rolled under him.

"Aaggh!" he cried in pain as he crumpled to the floor.

Instantly Mama was bending over him.

She peeled back Billy's sock and touched his ankle gently. Billy cried out again.

"Help me get him up," Mama said to Alexander. Together they lifted Billy onto a kitchen chair. The ankle was already starting to swell and turn a purplish colour. They propped it on another chair. Isobel fetched a pillow.

"It looks like a sprain," Mama said. "Alexander, get some ice from outside and wrap it in a clean cloth. We need to get this swelling down. Matt, there's a roll of bandages in the medicine box. Would you get it, please?" She looked sadly at Billy. "I'm afraid you won't be playing hockey today," she said.

Billy sat forward. "But I have to! We won't have enough players if I don't."

Mama shook her head. "You will never get your boot on, Billy, let alone your skate. If you put weight on your foot, you'll only make it worse."

Billy sagged back in his chair and looked glumly at his brothers. "What are we going to do?"

"We could play a man short," Freddie said. "There's no rule against it."

"Seneca could drop a player too," his twin pointed out. "Then it would be even. That's the fair thing to do."

"Which is why Seneca will never agree to do it. They're as good as champions right now."

"We can't just give up!" Billy exclaimed.

Mama patted his head and stood up. "You'll think of something, I'm sure. I'll be right back. I need to get my scissors to cut the bandage."

As soon as she was gone, Isobel gathered her brothers into a huddle. "I'll play in Billy's place," she whispered.

"But you can't," Matt whispered back. "You're a girl."

Isobel stubbornly stuck out her chin. "There's no rule about girls playing. Besides, I can dress like a boy. Billy and I are almost the same height. If I tuck my hair under my cap, no one will know I'm not him."

"But what about Papa?" Alexander said.

"It's an emergency," Billy declared. "Papa wouldn't want us to give up the championship without even trying."

Isobel looked into each of her brothers' eyes. When they didn't offer any more arguments, she said, "It's settled then."

She hurriedly pulled a pair of Billy's breeches on under her skirt.

When Mama returned, the children said they were heading out. They volunteered to take Billy to the game on the sled. When they were out of sight of the house, Isobel slipped her skirt off and hid it under the rug covering Billy's sled. Hopefully, people at the game would think she was Billy and he was her.

———•———

There was quite a crowd at the ice rink. The boys from the other teams all came, so the Harkness children left Billy with them. If Mama and Papa watched the game from the other end of the ice, Papa might think Isobel was with Billy. And if Mama figured out what was going on, Isobel hoped she wouldn't tell Papa.

Isobel was as excited and nervous as she could be, right up until the game got started. Then all she could think about was playing hockey.

She forgot about how big and tough the Seneca team was. And how she was the only girl. She didn't hear the crowd cheering. She didn't even see Mama and Papa arrive.

Mama's red woollen caps were a big help. At a glance, Isobel could see exactly where her brothers were. It made passing the puck a lot easier.

The Seneca and Ossington teams were well matched. Each side scored once in the first half and then again in the second. With time ticking down, the game was tied at two. It could go either way.

Isobel knew that this was when Seneca would start to pull dirty tricks. She had to be ready.

She was checking the boy named Harry. He was big and strong, but Isobel was quick and agile.

Seeing a chance to steal the puck, she stuck in her stick and scooped it away. Then she wheeled around and started towards Seneca's goal. She knew Harry would be right on her heels. And he was probably getting ready to trip her.

Isobel Stanley's words echoed in her head. *It's hard to hit a moving target.*

Isobel poured all the energy she had into her legs. "Faster, faster, faster," she told them. She could hear Harry's skates cutting into the ice behind her. Any second now he would stretch out his stick to catch her. It would come from the right, so Isobel quickly hopped to her left.

Out of the corner of her eye, she saw the blade of the stick sweep the ice where she had just been. Then she saw splotches of red on both sides of her. It was John and Freddie.

The goal was straight ahead. The goalkeeper was steeling himself for the shot. He was big. He took up almost all the space between the two posts that marked the goal. Isobel couldn't get a clear look. She saw John on her right. The goalkeeper saw her look and shifted his position slightly.

Then a stick slapped the ice to Isobel's left. In a blink, she passed the puck and watched as Freddie tucked it into the corner of the goal!

The whistle blew. The game was over.

Ossington had won.

PAPA HAS THE LAST WORD

Mama presented the cup, and everyone cheered. Well, everyone except the Seneca team.

Papa grinned from ear to ear as he clapped the boys on the back and congratulated them for their fine play.

But when he got to Isobel and realized she was the player who had taken Billy's place, his hand froze in mid-air. Instead of praising her, as he had the boys, he gulped so hard the Adam's apple in his throat jumped.

Isobel didn't know what to think. Papa certainly didn't seem pleased. But he wasn't scolding her for playing either. That was something to be thankful for.

When the family got home, Mama made supper while the children noisily relived the game.

Passing the kitchen, Isobel saw her parents with their heads together. They looked serious. She tiptoed past so she wouldn't disturb them. When she returned, Papa was gone.

"Supper," Mama finally called. "Go wash up." Then quietly to Isobel she said, "You tricked me, Isobel, though I have to say I wasn't really surprised to see you on the ice."

"I'm sorry," Isobel said. "Really, I am, Mama. But if you knew, you'd have told Papa, and he wouldn't have let me play."

Mama sighed and patted Isobel's head. "Speaking of Papa, he would like to speak with you. He is in the cellar."

Isobel's stomach did a somersault. Had she pushed Papa too far this time? Was she in big trouble? She looked into Mama's face for the answer, but it told her nothing.

"Go on," Mama urged her kindly. "Papa doesn't like to be kept waiting."

The trap door to the cellar was already open, so Isobel said a little prayer and started down the stairs. Right away, the cold air cut through her sweater, sending goosebumps up her arms.

The cellar was dark except for the lantern light in a far corner.

"Papa?" Isobel called, slowly padding towards the soft yellow glow. As she got closer, she was able to see Papa rummaging through a box.

"Aha!" he exclaimed. "Finally!" He looked up at Isobel, and his expression immediately became stern.

"Mama said you wanted to speak to me," Isobel said meekly. She steeled herself for a scolding.

Papa cleared his throat. "Yes, Isobel. I do."

Isobel took a deep breath and plunged in. No matter what punishment was in store for her, it was best to get it out of the way. "Is it about today's game?" she asked.

Papa frowned. "Yes, as a matter of fact, it is."

"I'm sorry," Isobel blurted. "I know you told me not to play, but the boys needed me, Papa. There was no one else, and I couldn't let them lose to Seneca without putting up a fight. I shouldn't have disobeyed you, but I really had no choice. As for playing with them when they practised, I was actually coaching, just—"

Papa put up a hand. "Isobel, stop."

Isobel closed her mouth and looked down at the floor.

"Yes, you disobeyed me, and I'm not happy about that. And you tricked your mother. I'm not happy about that either."

"I'm sorry, Papa," Isobel croaked. "Are you going to punish me?"

There was a pause before Papa replied. "I don't think that will be necessary. You already know you did wrong."

Isobel lowered her eyes again. "Yes, Papa."

Papa cleared his throat. "And, as your mother has pointed out to me, I may have been a bit unreasonable."

Isobel looked up and blinked in confusion.

Papa smiled. "The truth is I'm very proud of you, Isobel. You put the welfare of your brothers before yourself. Without you, the game would have been lost. You were as important to that team as anyone. I'm just sorry that you had to be sneaky to save the day."

Isobel's throat got tight, but she didn't know what to say anyway.

Papa continued, "I was wrong, Isobel. Girls should be allowed to play hockey if they want to. I'm sorry I was stubborn about that. You're right. Times are changing, and I must try to change with them. You are an excellent hockey player. I hope to watch you many more times. In fact, I hope you'll let me join you and your brothers in a game or two."

Isobel was still unable to speak, so she just nodded.

He dug inside the box again and pulled out a pair of skates. He grinned. "Of course, I'm a bit rusty."

"Oh, Papa!" Isobel exclaimed. "I'm sure you're not rusty at all. Mama said you are a fine skater."

Papa's eyes twinkled. "She did?"

Isobel nodded. "Yes, she did."

"Hmm." Papa pursed his lips in thought. "Do you think your mother might want to give hockey a try too?"

Isobel giggled. "You never know, Papa. You never know. Maybe we could start our very own Harkness family hockey team!"

AUTHOR'S NOTE

Isobel's Stanley Cup is a fun story, but it isn't true. None of the events actually happened—at least not that I know of. I made everything up. The characters aren't real either.

Except for one. Isobel Stanley really was the daughter of Lord Stanley, the Governor General of Canada in 1893, and she was passionate about hockey. She really did play on the rink at Rideau Hall. She wore a white skirt and jacket too. And the history books say she and her brothers were the ones who persuaded Lord Stanley to create an award for hockey.

I don't know if Isobel Stanley was still in Canada in 1893, and, of course, she and Isobel from the story never actually met, but wouldn't it have been wonderful if they had!

Isobel Stanley will always be remembered as a pioneer of women's hockey. Her married name was Isobel Gathorne-Hardy, and in 2000 the Isobel Gathorne-Hardy Award was created in her honour. Each year it is given to a player—at any level of hockey—whose personal qualities, values and leadership are a model for all female athletes.

Everything I wrote about the award that Lord Stanley created is true too. Today we call it the Stanley Cup, but it used to be called the Dominion Hockey Challenge Cup. It is awarded each year to the winning team of the National Hockey League (NHL). The cup looks quite different now, though. In fact, the original Dominion Challenge Cup is in the Hockey Hall of Fame (there's a photo at www.hhof.com—under "Stanley Cup Journal" in the top menu, click "Stanley Cup Journal Homepage"; then, at the bottom of that page, click "London England 2006"). Players now compete for a copy of the original bowl. It sits atop a stack of silver and nickel bands engraved with winners' names. The cup has grown taller and taller over the years as more and more champions are added to it. The Stanley Cup is now about 90 centimetres (35 inches) tall and weighs 15.5 kilograms (34 pounds). It won't get any larger, though, as the oldest bands are removed and moved to the Hall of Fame as new ones are added.

If you are a hockey fan, you will have noticed that hockey as Isobel and her brothers played it was a bit different from hockey today. In 1893 there were two equal periods of hockey instead of three, and there were seven players on the ice instead of six. There were no line changes back then either. Spare players only got into the game if someone were injured. And there was no hockey net—not even a crossbar—just two goalposts. There were also no hockey programs for young people, so kids had to organize and referee themselves.

And girls like Isobel really did have to push hard to be allowed to play. Thank goodness they didn't give up!

Women playing hockey in about 1890 in Ottawa. Isobel Stanley is wearing white.

Public Domain Photo. Title: Earliest known photograph of women playing hockey, taken at Rideau Hall, Ottawa, circa 1890.
Reference number: Proud past, bright future, *AMICUS No. 13669816, e011165573 McFarlane (Toronto, ON: Stoddart, 1994).*

ABOUT THE AUTHOR

Teacher-turned-writer Kristin Butcher has been creating books for children and young adults since 1997. *Isobel's Stanley Cup* is #26. Married to the Toronto Maple Leafs' staunchest fan, Kristin started watching hockey in self-defence, but somewhere along the line she got hooked and is now often the first one to turn on the game.